Happy Birthday, Sausage!

Michaela Morgan
Illustrated by Dee Shulman

A & C Black • London

First paperback edition 2011
First published 2010 by
A & C Black Publishers Ltd
36 Soho Square, London, W1D 3QY

www.acblack.com

Text copyright © 2010 Michaela Morgan
Illustrations copyright © 2010 Dee Shulman

The rights of Michaela Morgan and Dee Shulman to be identified
as the author and illustrator of this work has been asserted by them
in accordance with the Copyrights, Designs and Patents Act 1988.

ISBN 978-1-4081-2397-3

A CIP catalogue for this book is available from the British Library.

This book is produced using paper that is made from wood grown in
managed, sustainable forests. It is natural, renewable and recyclable.
The logging and manufacturing processes conform to the
environmental regulations of the country of origin.

Printed and bound in Singapore by Tien Wah Press (Pte) Ltd.

Chapter One

Would you like to meet a plump and
playful, loyal and loving, lovely, little
long dog? Here he is...

He looks a bit like a sausage.
His favourite food is … sausages.
And his friends and family call him …
guess what?

Fitz and Spatz, the two snooty cats,
share his home. But they don't really
like sharing.
And so they don't really like Sausage.
They call him…

5

The cats are never kind to Sausage.
Sometimes they *pretend* to be kind …

but really
they just like
to make
fun of him.

Sausage has lived with his family …

Jack

Elly

Hammy

and Gran →

for nearly one whole year.

7

And what a year it has been!

Sausage arrives.

Sleepover at the Spooky House.

JANUARY
FEBRUARY
MARCH
APRIL
MAY
JUNE
JULY
AUGUST
SEPTEMBER
OCTOBER
NOVEMBER
DECEMBER

Sausage captures burglars.

HOUND HERO!
A pair of robbers were stopped in their tracks by the brave and fearless Sausage!

Hammy comes to stay.

Sausage starts school.

Now it is November, which means it is nearly … Sausage's BIRTHDAY!

"I know," said Elly.

Chapter Two

"We can have balloons!" said Elly. "And sausages," thought Sausage.

Party food.

And sausages!

"We can have games!" said Jack.

And sausages!

"And a cake," said Gran.

With sausages?

13

Everyone was very excited.

Well … *nearly* everyone was very excited. Fitz and Spatz, the snooty cats, were not happy at all. They were jealous.
"All this fuss for one silly sausage dog!" they said.

Chapter Three

Elly and Jack started to
make the decorations
and the invitations.

Gran started planning the cake.

Sausage started choosing his birthday present.
He looked through the Party Animals catalogue.

"That's what I want," he thought.

Fitz and Spatz started their
skulking and sulking and
plotting and planning.

They were determined
to find a way of spoiling
the party.

Fitz sniggered. He sharpened his razor claws.

Spatz licked his lips

"I have a better idea," Fitz grinned.

Jack and Elly had a long list of
Sausage's friends:

Dusty

Spottydog

Tiny

Skcamp

Alfonso

Butch

Rex

Kevin

Lola

"They will all come to the party," said Elly. "Sausage is a very popular little dog."

Sausage smiled a little smile. It was a sausage-shaped smile.

Jack and Elly wrote out the invitations.

Please come to Sausage's party.
Friday at 2 o'clock
(Bring Sausages!)

Proudly, Sausage added the final touch –
his signature.

He took special care with Lola's
invitation. And he put something extra
on it – a great big red kiss.

Elly left all the invitations by the door. They were ready to be posted.
Then she went to help with the other preparations.
There was still a lot to do.

Chapter Four

Elly thought Gran had posted the invitations.

Gran thought Jack had posted the invitations.

Jack thought Elly had posted the invitations.

And Sausage thought *someone* had posted the invitations.

But here is what *really* happened…
Fitz and Spatz, the sneaky cats,
tiptoed into the hall …

grinned a nasty grin …

sniggered a sneaky snigger …

whispered,

and then they pushed all
the invitations into
a bin bag.

They dragged the bin bag outside
and left it by the door, ready to be
collected.

Sausage thought his invitations were on their way. He imagined his friends being excited and looking forward to his party. His head was full of happy party thoughts.

Even the cats seemed happy. They had
a twinkle in their eyes and a funny little
smile on their faces. They seemed to be
looking forward to the party, too.

The days passed slowly until, finally, it was ... party day!

At two o'clock, Sausage stood by the window, waiting for his friends. He was looking forward to a brilliant party.

Time went on … and not one of his guests turned up. The only people who came to his street were the bin men coming to pick up the rubbish and the recycling.

Sausage had no cards. No presents. No friends. And, worst of all … no Lola. A big tear ran down his face.

Chapter Five

Outside in the
street, the bin
men continued
with their work.

Dan, the recycling man, was feeling
a bit cross.

"So much of this stuff could be recycled," he said.
He picked up a bin bag with a pile of letters in it and threw them in his truck.
"Woof!" agreed Dusty, his dog.

Suddenly, Dusty dived into the back of the truck and came out with a letter that was addressed to him.
"I never knew you could read, Dusty," said Dan.

"Woof!" said Dusty.
He shook the dust from his paws and
jumped down from the truck.

But Dan the recycling man stopped him.
"No, Dusty," he said. "You can't go to
the party … we have work to do."

Dusty and Dan got into the truck and drove away.

Chapter Six

All that afternoon,
Sausage waited
and waited...

The two bad cats sniggered and sneered
and sang a nasty song.

Sausage was the saddest little sausage
dog in the whole wide world.

And then …
over the hill to the rescue came …
Ta Da!

Dan the recycling man and his not-so-dusty dog.

Dusty was all cleaned up and ready for the party and so were all the other dogs. Lola was looking particularly lovely.

"We found your invitations – and we delivered them," Dan explained. "We've brought your guests and we've brought you a present."

Chapter Seven

What a party!
There was fine food to eat…

Dances to
dance…

Hats to wear…

There were games
to play…

Songs to sing…

And, of course … presents!

Sausage was given rubber balls, strings of sausages, new clothes, a juicy bone – and the big bouncy birthday banana.

The cats sneered at the presents and tossed them to one side.

Then it was time for the cake.
Gran came in with it …

and everyone started singing.

Then …

it all went bananas!

Sausage and his doggy friends had a wonderful time. They all agreed it was a perfect party! And everyone thought the cake was fantastic! Well … *nearly* everyone.